Copyright © Tony Ross, 2006
The rights of Tony Ross to be identified as the author and illustrator of this work
have been asserted by him in accordance with the Copyright, Designs and Patents Act, 1988.
First published in Great Britain in 2006 by Andersen Press Ltd, 20 Vauxhall Bridge Road,
London SW1V 2SA. Published in Australia by Random House Australia Pty.,
20 Alfred Street, Milsons Point, Sydney, NSW 2061. All rights reserved.
Colour separated in Switzerland by Photolitho AG, Zürich.
Printed and bound in Italy by Grafiche AZ, Verona.

10   9   8   7   6   5   4   3   2   1

British Library Cataloguing in Publication Data available.

ISBN-10: 1 84270 585 7
ISBN-13: 978 1 84270 585 8

This book has been printed on acid-free paper

I Want To Go Home!

Tony Ross

Andersen Press
London

One day, the Queen found a new castle.

"This one's too small, now we have your brother!"

"And then, there's that lot," she said.

"And THAT LOT . . ."
"I don't want to live somewhere else,"
said the Little Princess.

"Oh, yes you do," said the Queen.
"You'll have much more room."

So, the Duke of Somewhereorother
bought the old castle . . .

. . . and the Little Princess moved into the new one.

"I WANT TO GO HOME!" said the Little Princess.

"You ARE home," said the Queen. "Look at your posh new room. It's big, and full of your things."

"I WANT TO GO HOME!" said the Little Princess.

"But look at the new garden," said the Queen.
"Perhaps the Gardener will let you help him."

"I WANT TO GO HOME!" said the Little Princess.

"But look at the new kitchen," said the Queen.
"I want to go home NOW!" said the Little Princess.

"Very well," said the Queen. "You can go back
to the old castle, but only for a peep."

"The Duke of Somewhereorother lives there now. Look, he's painted it!"

"The Dukelet lives in your old room!"

"Look at the lovely new kitchen!"
said the Duchess of Somewhereorother.

"And see how nice the garden is
without those horrible trees . . ."

"We could have tea and cake on the lawn . . .

. . . so long as you don't drop crumbs."

"After all, we don't want birds, do we? I have
to hoover the grass every day as it is."

"I WANT TO GO HOME!" said the Little Princess.
"ME TOO!" said the Queen.

"Mmmmmmmmm!" said the Little Princess.
"This is more like it!"

Other *Little Princess* Picture Books

Little Princess Board Books: